HOW MANY SLEEPS 'til my Birthday?

by
Mark Sperring

Illustrated by
Sébastien Braun

tiger tales

One summer morning, when the birds were busy
waking the world with a song, Little Pip climbed out of bed,
padded across the floor, and . . .

"PSSST!" He gave Daddy Grizzle a BIG bear shake. "Daddy Grizzle, WAKE UP!" said Little Pip. "Today is a very special day."

"That's nice," mumbled Daddy Grizzle.

"Yes," said Little Pip, "because today is my birthday!"
(For a moment, the birds fell silent.)

Then

THUD, he jumped out of bed and dashed out the door.

"But WAIT," said Daddy Grizzle. "Today isn't your birthday. There are still THREE whole sleeps 'til your birthday."

"Really . . .?" sighed Little Pip.

"Really," nodded Daddy Grizzle, "but seeing that we're up, let's go out anyway."

So out they went into the woods and carefully collected some branches and twigs.

That night, tucked in tight,
Little Pip thought he heard
the *scrape* of a saw and the
tap of a hammer before . . .

ZZZZZZZZ

he fell fast asleep.

The next morning, when Daddy Grizzle was still snoozing,
Little Pip gave him a shake.

"PSSST! Wake up, Daddy Grizzle!" he said.
"I think it's my birthday!"

Daddy Grizzle's eyes
POPPED open.

Then he threw off his blanket,

grabbed a basket . . .

and *rushed* out the door.

But as soon as he had gone outside,
Daddy Grizzle remembered something VERY important,
and with a BIG bear GROAN, he turned around and
headed back inside.

"*No*, Little Pip," sighed Daddy Grizzle, "today is NOT your birthday. In fact, there are **TWO whole sleeps** until your birthday."

"Really . . . ?" sighed Little Pip.

"**Really**," sighed Daddy Grizzle,
"but now that we're up, let's go out anyway."

So out they went and filled their baskets with all the
most beautiful things the woods had to offer.

When they got home later that day,
Daddy Grizzle reminded Little Pip just
how many sleeps there were until his birthday.

And that night, as Little Pip stirred
from the sweetest of dreams,
he thought he caught a *whiff* of
something wonderful before . . .

ZZZZzzzzz^{zzz}

falling back to sleep.

The next day, Little Pip (what a clever bear) *somehow* remembered it was NOT his birthday that day.

little Pip,
GO back to sleep.
It's **NOT** your birthday,
thanks
Daddy Grizzle xxx

But "PSSST!" he still had a
very important question to ask . . . .

"Daddy Grizzle! Daddy Grizzle!
HoW MaNy SLeEpS
             'til my birthday?"

Daddy Grizzle rose
sleepily from his pillow.
"Little Pip," he yawned,
"only ONE more sleep to go."

DIY
D

And seeing as they were both awake now,
             they got up and went out . . . .

And while Little Pip kept himself busy with all sorts of things, Daddy Grizzle handed out some very important invitations.

That night, before bed, Little Pip was bursting with excitement. "How many sleeps 'til my birthday?" he asked.

"One," whispered Daddy Grizzle. "Just one."

POP

And as Little Pip drifted off to sleep,

ZZZZZZZZZZ

he thought he heard a little POp.

The following morning,
Little Pip knew EXACTLY
what day it was.

But when he went to wake up Daddy Grizzle,
all he found was a note . . . .

So Little Pip followed the balloons out of the house, down the path . . .

He followed them into the woods, through the stream, SPLiSh! SPLaSh! SPLoSh!

. . . and over the bridge.

And right past the berry bushes—WhOoPs! PoP!—until . . .

Well, Little Pip couldn't have wished for a better surprise or a nicer birthday. All of his friends were there, and everything was perfect!

And later . . . much later, when the cake
had been eaten and the games had been played,
Little Pip dashed around laughing and playing
with his friends and new toys.

"Who knows...," said Daddy Grizzle.
"Tomorrow morning we might even
get to SLEEP IN. *How nice.*"

But the next morning, before the birds had even sung
a single note, a little voice said loudly,

"PSSST! Daddy Grizzle!
Daddy Grizzle!

the end

or is it?

one...

two...

For Louise with much and many thanks – M. S.

To Cath, the best party organizer ever – S. B.

tiger tales
5 River Road, Suite 128, Wilton, CT 06897
Published in the United States 2016
Originally published in Great Britain 2013
by Puffin Books
Text copyright © 2013 Mark Sperring
Illustrations copyright © 2013 Sébastien Braun
ISBN-13: 978-1-68010-009-9
ISBN-10: 1-68010-009-2
Printed in China
10 9 8 7 6 5 4 3 2 1

For more insight and activities, visit us at www.tigertalesbooks.com